WHITE RUNS THE ALMOND TREE

A PLAY

BY

MILO ADDAMS

WILD CENTURIES PRESS

WILD CENTURIES PRESS
www.wildcenturies.com

Copyright © 2012 WILD CENTURIES PRESS

ISBN-10: 0983584532

ISBN-13: 978-0-9835845-3-7

Typefaces: Times Roman, Gill Sans MT

...when the almond tree blossoms...
people go to their eternal home...
Ecclesiastes 12:5 [NIV]

CAST OF CHARACTERS

EDDIE   famous writer, also called 'Pops' or 'lamb'.

MAGGIE   Eddie's wife; also a writer.

L.C.   Eddie's colleague and friend, also a writer.

DRAKE   psychiatrist with patients at St. Martha's.

GRACE   nurse at St. Martha's hospital.

BERTHA   nurse at St. Martha's hospital.

PRIEST   Roman Catholic priest at St. Martha's.

SETTING

The action takes place in 1961 at St. Martha's, just one hospital that serves a renowned clinic in the Midwest. The United States recently jumped a generation to elect a young president with style and vision; he reads Ian Fleming.

ACT ONE
Eddie's private hospital room mid-morning in June.

ACT TWO
Doctor Drake's office later that morning.

ACT THREE
Eddie private hospital room that afternoon.

WHITE RUNS THE ALMOND TREE

ACT ONE

Eddie's room. Stage left is oblique wall with large French doors (with no panes) USL. Through the closed but revealing doors sits a metal cart rife in hospital corridors. A messy food tray tops the cart. Near less oblique wall SR is desk and chair DSR. Lording the desk is a large white bust of Shakespeare wearing a dark knit skullcap. USR is a wheelchair. Between the wheelchair and a narrow hospital bed USC is a window with pulled drapes. Fronting the window is a tray table on rollers. Taped and pinned to the US wall between the bed and the window are dozens of papers and photographs. The SR wall has a door open USR and a door closed DSR. EDDIE, with white hair and white beard, barefoot in a Masai-orange robe, stands bouncy and square-shouldered at the tray table and writes furiously. A long scroll of paper covered in writing dangles off US side of the tray table and virgin paper dangles off the DS side and connects to a roll of toilet paper on the floor. EDDIE steps back agile as a cat and peeks through the drapes. He returns to the tray table, glares at his stub of a pencil and throws it in a wastebasket by his feet. He pulls a new pencil from a robe pocket.

EDDIE (*in gruff, macho voice*): Well, Bill Shakespeare, (*salutes bust on desk*) three whole goddamn number twos. (*pulls out a pocket knife to sharpen new pencil*) Old days before I could afford a pencil sharpener, could whittle through six number twos every goddamn morning. Not Sunday morning. Bad luck to write on Sunday. Three number twos not bad for this chickenshit joint though. Had black ass for hour and a half too. Oatmeal laced with enough barbiturates to send King Kong into nosedive. Had to hock Hathaway future to Nurse Bertha to get this little shiv. Couldn't castrate Truman Capote's cat with it. (*admires point on pencil and pounces to French doors USL to look and listen, then bounds to drapes to peek out again*) Goddamn, Bill! (*to bust of Shakespeare*) It's a goddamn invasion!

(EDDIE springs to the tray table, wads up paper into huge armload, runs DSR to open closet door and throws mess on floor over two suitcases and one pair of shoes. Two white guayaberas, two leather vests and a pair of baggy tweed pants hang on closet bar. He slams the door, runs to turn off the lights by doors USL and races USR to sit in the wheelchair. L.C. and MAGGIE appear well illuminated through the French doors. They walk arm in arm but then quickly separate. She leaned so heavily he seems relieved. L.C. is about forty, dressed like a college professor in horn-rimmed glasses and plaid sport coat with leather elbows. MAGGIE is mature, with tailored clothes and light summer fur that warn she is no one to be trifled with. They pause and whisper to each other before MAGGIE taps on door and enters the room. L.C. backs off and stands idly behind the cart.)

2

MAGGIE (*softly*): Eddie? (*turns on lights*) There you are, Eddie darling.

EDDIE (*in a meek, hollow voice*): Who is it?

MAGGIE (*walks to the wheelchair*): Don't you know it's me, lamb?

EDDIE: I didn't ring for nurse. Go away. Dark so peaceful...

MAGGIE (*kisses his cheek*): Eddie, don't you know it's me? It's Maggie.

EDDIE: Miss Maggie! I was so relaxed. Dark so peaceful. So nice.

MAGGIE (*soft spoken but very suspicious*): Yes, darling.

EDDIE: Had another treatment yesterday, dear. Treatments helped son Patrick too, you know. Remember old kraut doc Stetski in Cuba? The firm is slow today...but tranquil as frost-bitten dawn in Idaho.

  (L.C. intently examines the food tray, pulls out a small notebook and begins to scribble, obviously upset with himself for not doing it sooner.)

MAGGIE (*putters around bed*): Don't you know it's June, lamb?

EDDIE: (*irritably*) Yes, It's June! (*forcing civility*) I mean I'm feeling very relaxed, almost like the time in...oh, what's the name of that joint? You know, mountain top near Madrid...whats-his-name's cave is there! No, no.

More peaceful yet. Over by...by Pamplona! Northeast I think. The...oh, what the hell is that river?

MAGGIE (*impatient, expecting L.C. to enter*): Where that strange dog bolted out and scared me half to death? Don't you remember it was the Irati River?

EDDIE: Irati! That doesn't sound quite right. Anyway, it was some river somewhere near...what did I just say? Pamplona? (*to Shakespeare*) Major part of one of my big ones. Seemed peaceful there once in some forest.

MAGGIE (*glancing at the door*): Do you think so, darling?

    (L.C. stuffs the notebook inside his coat and knocks on the door.)

EDDIE: Friend or enema?

MAGGIE: Enter, please!

L.C. (*enters tentatively*): Pops?

EDDIE (*holds up hand*): Don't interrupt me. I can make him. This is important. I have always made things stick that I wanted to stick. Don't interrupt! Not one gray hair in well-coiffed head. Must be young chickenshit purveyor of half-real people in half-real world. Trilling? Bellow? James Jones? Mailer? (*to Shakespeare*) Jack them all up and you have nothing. This boy ogles me with real fondness, with a cat's smile...

MAGGIE: Now Eddie...

L.C.: Pops, it's your old tout, L.C.

EDDIE (*claps his hands*): Oh, hell. Don't I know old L.C.?
Better than old black dog? (*frowns*) Wait! Goddamn it. I
think something bad happened to black dog.

MAGGIE: Eddie, please. L.C., I'm so startled to see you.

L.C.: Oh! (*walks over to hug her*) Grand to see you,
Maggie.

EDDIE: Got to work on lackluster greetings. No wonder
L.C. with a fistful of greenbacks can't fornicate a
starving whore.

> (with effort EDDIE stands and he and L.C. try to
> wrap left arms around each other's shoulders and
> slap their backs while they shake right hands)

L.C.: Just like Autcuil, laying francs on the nags!

EDDIE: Somebody here...I remember now. Hot one here
for L.C. I'll remember name in a minute. What was I
talking about? Oh. I have hot one here for L.C. Breasts
stuffed tighter than sausages.

MAGGIE (*moves over behind the wheelchair*): L.C., what
brings you here?

L.C.: I just wanted to shoot the breeze a bit. Like we
did...we do at Harry's Bar...or Floridita.

EDDIE: A breeze is a hurricane in this chickenshit joint.
(*sits down again*) I've found perfect peace here.

> (MAGGIE gently combs and primps EDDIE's hair.
> He is visibly irritated but says nothing.)

5

L.C.: I wanted to pass on a few ball scores.

EDDIE: No bean balls. What is angular angler Theodore Williams batting? Goddamn, what a grooved swing! Never bunted that I saw. Knocked the shift on its ass.

L.C.: Longshot named Maris is making a run on the Babe.

EDDIE: I'll be in a fine and secret place before anybody catches the Babe.

L.C.: Floyd Patterson signed to fight a Tom McNeeley.

EDDIE: That whisper of wind won't destroy my serenity. (*frowns*) Goddamn it, didn't I win a bundle of dough betting against Patterson once? By Christ, I wonder if I reported that as income...

L.C.: I guess you heard about the Bay of Pigs gamble.

EDDIE (*genuinely distressed*): Lost the finca. Goddamn, miss boat too. Shit-maru! I remember now! That Batista mob beat old black dog to death. Beat his old blind brains out.

L.C.: Sorry, Pops. I guess I shouldn't...

MAGGIE (*angrily puts the comb in her pocket*): That's all right! (*pointedly*) Eddie can take bad news...

EDDIE: Jammed a lifetime of goddamned little else into my books. A million words. (*to Shakespeare*) True words!

L.C. (*sits on edge of bed close to EDDIE*): I better just shut up and deal. Just get it out. You like it that way, Pops.

EDDIE (*looks at crotch of L.C.*): You got a bum rap on me from some wishful chickenshit professor. I'm fond of women even if most are sick as hell. No. Don't get it out.

MAGGIE: Listen to him, Eddie...please.

L.C.: What I meant was I want to lay it on the line.

EDDIE: No better place to lay it as on the line.

L.C.: Stretch cashed in.

EDDIE: Stretch? Goddamn it. He said he'd beat me to the barn.

L.C.: Cancer. Of the prostate. Pops, I saw him just before he died...

EDDIE: Let me remember it! All these chickenshit medicos couldn't erase a true pal like Stretch. Don't interrupt me! Stretch. Honest and straight and friendly and unspoiled. For an actor too, which runs about as miraculous as the transfiguration. Goddamn good times together. Damn good shot. Tight about dough as a hog's ears in flytime.

MAGGIE: I'm afraid that's why L.C. came...

L.C.: Sure. Pops, I saw Stretch just before he died...

EDDIE: (*depressed*): I heard you the first time. If you get the words right you don't have to say it again. (*quick glance at Shakespeare*)

7

L.C.: I just mean I got to talk to him. He asked me to tell you something...

EDDIE: Thanks for clarification. Stretch is dead. Cancer.

L.C.: About what he said up in Idaho that time. About...

EDDIE: I remember! He was apologetic as a menstruating whore.

MAGGIE: Eddie, listen to him.

L.C.: Stretch just wanted to make sure you knew he thought he finally dealt himself a good hand.

EDDIE: Good. He can balance this failed Catholic. Goddamn it though. I'm going to miss Stretch. It wasn't his fault those plaster Zanucks transformed two of my best books into celluloid manure. Stretch...

MAGGIE: Staying here is really doing wonders for Eddie.

L.C.: I see that. He looks like three to five against the field.

MAGGIE: With the right kind of professional care he's got the old furnace going.

L.C.: Hot as a tip from a jockey.

EDDIE: Euphemistically speaking, Miss Maggie wants me to stay here. Maybe until the furnace goes out...

MAGGIE: Eddie, please. It's just that staying here is doing you so much good.

L.C. (*doubtfully*): You are looking first rate, Pops. But maybe you should cool the old Sancerre a little longer...

EDDIE: Sancerre? (*enthused*) I remember now. Crackling cold. Understood. All peacefully bottled up in a nice green bottle. Submerged in nice peaceful ice...like ice in an iceberg...bottom of which is like all the stuff (*to Shakespeare*) I left out of my stories.

> (DRAKE appears USL outside the French doors. He wears a white coat. A stethoscope hangs on his neck. He scans the room.)

L.C.: That's the old charger Pops. Like Epinard!

MAGGIE: That's the young Eddie.

EDDIE: That's peaceful Edward Hathaway. Tranquil. Serene. Blissful. Floating in a fog of pharmaceuticals.

> (DRAKE finally knocks, very loud.)

MAGGIE: Enter, please.

DRAKE: And how is our Mr. Jones doing today?

MAGGIE: I'm afraid he's...(*suddenly stops*)

DRAKE (*extends hand to L.C.*): I'm Dr. Drake. I don't believe we've met...

L.C.: I'm L.C. Mankin, Doctor...

DRAKE: Fellow...

EDDIE: Writer!

DRAKE: L.C...

EDDIE: Lower case!

DRAKE: (*phony chuckle*) I see. How are we today, Mr. Jones?

> (L.C. moves USL and watches EDDIE carefully now.)

EDDIE: Relaxed. Peaceful. Tranquil. Serene. Speaking for my Jones half. And your half?

DRAKE: You sound solid as the door on a Duesenberg.

EDDIE (*contemptuously to Shakespeare*): Stretch had a Duesenberg from his pocket change. I had to cut my veins to get a Packard.

DRAKE: Yes, Mr. Jones, you do appear quite relaxed.

MAGGIE: Doctor, have you read Eddie's book on bullfighting yet?

DRAKE: I started it...

EDDIE: Started it! (*seeing MAGGIE withdraw, he calms himself*) Perhaps you could expand that thought, doc...

DRAKE: I'm not into that...sort of thing much.

EDDIE: (*glowering sulkily at Shakespeare*): What thing is that?

DRAKE: Well, you see, I'm an animal lover.

MAGGIE: Eddie wrote a beautiful book on Africa and all
the animals.

DRAKE: I'm not keen on hurting...I mean hunting animals.
I liked his book on the skipper that joined the resistance
to fight the Nazis...

MAGGIE: Really, doctor? Which part?

DRAKE: Oh, all of it. It was fine.

MAGGIE: Really, doctor? All of it?

EDDIE (*benignly*): What's wrong with that? I wrote all of
it. (*eyes DRAKE's brown shoes*) Doc, that is one swell
pair of winged tips. Been searching for a pair of brogues
like that for biped Edward Jones. (*L.C. and MAGGIE
exchange knowing looks*) My foot gear are flaps of elk
hide suited to no one but Indian. Your shoes massive.
Each must preserve three pounds of cow. Reek of much
dough. How much moolah, doc?

DRAKE (*suspicious*): I don't recall how much money,
precisely. Just thought I would look in for a moment.
(*stops at door USL*) Mr. Jones looks solid as sterling.

EDDIE: I'm not running as silver or cordovan right now.
Ebony good color for hooves of Edward Jones. But
might need loan. Don't interrupt me. I can get a make on
them. Rugged imports. Keith Highlanders. Sixty,
seventy dollars a pair. By Christ though, I could tromp
anywhere in those shoes. Maybe kick down wall of
Havana whorehouse. Maybe if L.C. had shoes like that...

DRAKE: I'll be in my office, Mrs. Hath... Jones.

> (DRAKE leaves and walks offstage USL, shaking his head as if he is very glad to escape.)

EDDIE (*boiling but trying not to show it*): So he liked one of my books...

L.C.: So that's your Doctor Drake?

EDDIE: You observed stethoscope necklace too?

MAGGIE: Eddie...

> (GRACE comes onstage USL, knocks on French doors but walks in immediately. Her breasts are large, unnaturally high and very pointed. Otherwise she is trim in neat white uniform, shoes and cap. She frequently smoothes her uniform.)

Well, enter, please.

EDDIE: Even if you don't please. But please do.

GRACE: Mr. Hath...I mean Mr. Jones, you look like you sucked the seeds from a lemon. You just stay relaxed now.

EDDIE: No problem, Grace. Grace! That's the name I couldn't remember for sausages. But I am relaxed. How about you, L.C.? Are you relaxed when you see Nurse Grace?

MAGGIE: Eddie, please...

GRACE: Oh, Mr. Jones and I tickle each other. (*putters around EDDIE, straightening his robe with disinterest as if he is very old man*) There now. (*poking at his right side with real interest*) Liver still swollen? My, yes! And how you finger up this chair! (*flicks fingers in disgust against owl*)

EDDIE: I feel so peaceful now. Nurse Grace and Doc Drake work in tandem, spreading tranquility like soft dusk before the dark. How about reading my blood vessels, nurse?

GRACE (*moves on to straighten bed*): You can see I don't have the proper equipment. But Mr. Jones is always such a old gentleman. So relaxed...

EDDIE: Double-talk for no physical relationship. But, honestly now, L.C., what do you think of my Florence Nightingale's astounding milk glands?

MAGGIE: Eddie, please...

GRACE: Oh, I'm not touched by such rude remarks. (*nastily*) In Mr. Jones' case I know there's nothing behind it. Is your inflamed skin better on your nose and cheeks, Mr. Jones? Still pustular? Flaking? The alarming redness is about the same I think.

EDDIE: Honestly now, L.C., other than the Alps, have you ever seen peaks invade the clouds like those protrusions?

MAGGIE: Now, Eddie...

GRACE: I'd love to see Mr. L.C. use his lips.

L.C.: She just came out of the paddock but I'm in love with her eyes. They're so bright, so alert.

GRACE: Thank you. I should give you a real squeeze.

EDDIE (*to Shakespeare*): Bullshit and ruined with adjective. But good enough for a Grace.

MAGGIE: Grace is an angel to put up with you, Eddie.

GRACE (*goes inside door USR*): Mr. Jones and I have a feel for each other now and there's nothing between us and couldn't be...

EDDIE: Nurse must have bed pans to boss.

GRACE (*comes out door USR carrying a small paper cup*): Yes, I must go. (*reaching inside her uniform pocket*) Just as soon as Mr. Jones massages down one little pill.

EDDIE: No doubt to prevent me from splitting impertinence up to ivory throat...

MAGGIE: Eddie, relax, lamb...

GRACE (*viciously*): He is relaxed. He's going to snuggle those tired old wornout limbs into his chair and he's going to stay relaxed.

L.C.: Pops, perhaps I should sit out a while.

EDDIE (*carefully puts pill in mouth and swallows water*): Goddamned near choked on that golf ball. Grace's dank well worn treasure is safe again.

GRACE: A thousand times over in your case. You just cuddle up in your chair now and relax.

(GRACE minces out French doors, exits USR.)

L.C.: Quite a substantial nurse.

EDDIE: She could give a dutiful and wooden ride but nurse is key word. Some kind of record mammary to total body weight ratio.

MAGGIE: Relax, Eddie.

EDDIE: I am, Miss Maggie. Pill numbed me, noggin to gonads.

L.C.: Maybe you should sit out one race, Pops. Rest.

EDDIE: You can usually find her grazing near Doc Drake. Ride her once very well for me.

(L.C. walks outside French doors, waits.)

MAGGIE: Sleepy, darling?

EDDIE: Yes. Go eat poached egg, dear. Got worked up a bit. Kind of remembering but not remembering. Which is the way I run in this joint. I'm okay now. Feel peaceful. Happy to be alive.

MAGGIE: (*suspiciously*) I think I will eat. I'm afraid I had no breakfast.

EDDIE: You've got to keep your strength up. Not easy fussing around a tranquil old guy in a wheelchair all day.

MAGGIE: Later, darling.

EDDIE: Mind killing light, Miss Maggie? These
    chickenshit pills are resurrecting my keratosis sicca.
    Eyes oversensitized, genitals dormant.

MAGGIE: Do rest a while, lamb.

EDDIE: Just kill the light...

> (MAGGIE leaves without turning off lights, meets
> L.C. outside French doors and arm in arm they
> stroll offstage USL. EDDIE jumps up from the
> wheelchair to rant at Shakespeare.)

Goddamn medico! Doesn't like hurting animals. Maybe
I kill animals so I won't kill him. Maybe better to kill
fifty million goddamn rabbits than to kill fifty million
people which we just did. Does he think I have never
been shot at? Two years longer than Ulysses Grant is
all! I do nothing that was not done to me. Goddamn it, I
got shot and I was crippled and I got away. (*peeks out
drapes*) What do I have in this joint to kill? No,
goddamn it, I didn't want to think that. Oatmeal wore
off. I beat the black ass. Think what else doc said. He
saw that awful Bogey movie! Goddamn movie wasn't
even in my book. (*very agitated, pulls pill out of mouth*)

> (BERTHA, a rotund nurse, pads onstage USL. She
> is dressed like GRACE and she pushes a cart loaded
> with towels and supplies for rooms. She stops by
> French doors, hangs a stethoscope around her neck
> and takes from the cart a blood pressure gauge with
> cuff and a tiny tray with two paper cups.)

16

And that Grace! Fit for idiot permanently arrested at suckling stage! As if Hathaway would have physical need for guernsey! And carrying that name Grace, by Christ. Sweet mother Grace. (*in high-pitched voice*) Here, Edward, I thought you'd like to have as a Christmas present the revolver your father killed himself with. (*normal raspy voice*) Goddamn it, I didn't want to think about that. I beat the black ass...

> (BERTHA walks into the room with the tiny tray and the blood-pressure gauge. EDDIE stuffs the pill in his robe pocket.)

Bountiful Bertha!

BERTHA: If it aint Doctor Hathenstein...I mean Mr. Jones.

> (PRIEST, in black suit, black dickie and white collar, wanders onstage USL. He looks warily through open French doors.)

EDDIE (*loud but cautious*): Still at odds with our mutual adversary Drake?

BERTHA: Aint I always? (*sets her equipment on the tray table and motions EDDIE to the bed*) Move your heinie over here. Grace said you have to gobble up all of them pills.

> (PRIEST seems to notice BERTHA, exits USL.)

EDDIE (*sits on edge of bed, pushes up sleeve on right arm*): Request granted. (*salutes*) Wanted to identify your flag first. Couldn't be happier than French whore on D-Day. Always eager to take on doctor.

17

BERTHA (*adjusting cuff on arm*): You wouldn't of seen no Doctor Drake choking down spam on Omaha beach.

EDDIE: Too young?

> (BERTHA puts stethoscope in her ears, places end in crook of EDDIE's arm and pumps up the cuff.)

BERTHA: Too young! He wasn't gumming no pablum that day. He's forty.

EDDIE: Even a doctor can't help it if his feet are flat although not many stiffs being culled in that war.

BERTHA (*stops pumping*): Why do you think he went into psychiatry?

EDDIE (*watching process intently*): Dough for shoes.

BERTHA (*after pause of ten seconds*): One thirty-six over ninety-four. Shoes? You writers are funny. No, Drake don't have no stomach for blood. (*takes the cuff off and EDDIE rushes to the wall on the other side of the bed*) I think he's always chewing on my heinie because he knows I could wolf down a jelly donut standing in blood up to my knees. He knows I was over there in Korea.

EDDIE: Only goddamned war I missed.

BERTHA: Drake won't do nothing serious to me. He knows I would beat the stuffing out of him.

EDDIE (*jotting on scrap of paper thumbtacked to wall*): One thirty-six over ninety-four. Plenty good reason not to do anything to you.

BERTHA: Anyways, I told you, he's got enough woman trouble. Did you get enough grub for breakfast?

EDDIE: Half a zebra and two warthogs. Four wives made me wise on that woman rap.

BERTHA: Four wives? You using the can okay?

EDDIE: Hathaway raining dung at will. Four wives of which third was bad mistake. Countless other intimate contacts, both consummated and unconsummated.

BERTHA: You writers...

EDDIE: A man who suffers from a woman has disease more incurable than cancer. It's being sick herself that makes a woman act so goddamned badly. Wonder if I put that in a book?

BERTHA (*straightening bed*): You writers...

EDDIE: Knew some damned fine women that I never even touched.

BERTHA: Including my tenderloins.

EDDIE: That's only temporary. But remember two women especially fine. Actresses but never held that against them. One Kraut who defines dramatic pause and one Swede who refuses to call me Pops. Need for Hathaway blazes in their eyes brighter than Times Square. My eyes incandesce with willingness too. But passion never synchronizes. When they are available I am not. When I am available they are not. Or when all are estranged, all too burned out from prior arrangements.

19

BERTHA (*glancing into the wastebasket*): Well, I missed a few of them picnics myself.

EDDIE: Generals and privates and chaplains. Goddamn! Spill it, Bertha. Don't leave out one goddamned true word.

BERTHA: And have you write it up so any fool can snack on it?

EDDIE: Tell me about Nurse Grace and the well-shod doctor again.

BERTHA (*tidying up his desk*): I already fed you that morsel.

EDDIE: Did I ever tell you about that Italian Venus that goddamned near got me bumped off?

BERTHA: No. (*looks around*) Did I drag them in here or not?

EDDIE: Rounded in all places. She even had bottoms of eyes rounded. We did it every way possible. Fifteen times we did do it on a grand piano while I played Beethoven with my toes and recited Jack Donne.

BERTHA (*distracted*): You did...

> (She walks out French doors and putters with the towels on the cart. EDDIE immediately pounces to the drapes.)

EDDIE (*peeking and yelling*): Anyway, I found out just in time she belonged to Legs Diamond...

BERTHA (*yelling*): I heard of that butcher all right.

EDDIE (*still peeking and yelling*): Also ran into Mata Hari once. Said she read me and liked my stuff okay and wanted to show me what she did best. She started good but she got more interested in what was happening to her than what was happening to me which was goddamned tragic for me.

(EDDIE strolls coolly away from window just as BERTHA walks back in the room with two towels.)

BERTHA: Now all of St. Martha's right down to them hashers in the cafeteria knows it was tragic.

EDDIE: I know you won't treat me so badly.

BERTHA: You just have to promise me not to scream the results to the Chicago stockyards.

EDDIE: Danced all night once at Le Jockey in Paris, right after alleged first world war. Partner was woman with coffee skin and ebony eyes and naked breasts under black fur that bounced that fur like it was fine silk.

BERTHA: Coffee?

EDDIE: Two goddamned wars before I dived back into melting pot again - in Africa with Wakamba bride of eighteen. (*walks to picture on wall US*) Lovely, isn't she? Found out I inherited her seventeen year old widowed sister. As trio, we did it very well in goatskin bed fourteen feet across and not one inch too wide.

BERTHA: You writers...

21

EDDIE: Not room left in bed for one careless lizard dropping off thatched ceiling.

BERTHA: Lizard!

EDDIE: Am fond of lizards too.

BERTHA: I better not turn my backside on you.

EDDIE: Going to bathe me? Hope you brought good supply of towels. (*bounces on feet like a boxer*) Feel quite virile.

BERTHA (*shows him two towels as she walks through door USL*): Aint you always just fresh as an apple?

EDDIE: Two towels? Not enough to dry the Hathaway howitzer.

BERTHA (*yelling from inside his bathroom USR*): Say! Are you still using alcohol for them sponge baths?

EDDIE: Are you about through in the can? Have you obliterated all signs of carnal rampage?

BERTHA: You writers.

EDDIE: What lovemaking shall we invent today? I especially like it when you straddle me and plant right foot on Hathaway chin, then push off to gyroscope on my pole of pulsating plenitude...

> (PRIEST appears outside French doors, looks for a moment, then pokes head in door. EDDIE enthusiastically but silently waves him in.)

22

BERTHA (*still yelling from inside bathroom*): I don't need no dictionary to know that would be the last foolish act of Doctor Hathenstein. Don't never take no baby spoon to a banquet. There wouldn't be enough of your pecker left to feed a flea.

EDDIE: What has that to do with the prayer vigil I maintain for Pope John the twenty-third? We must pray the Second Vatican Council carries out God's true plan...

PRIEST: What did you say, my son?

BERTHA (*still inside the bathroom*): You don't sound right. If you writers aint a funny bunch of fritters.

EDDIE: I pray constantly for divine intercession...

BERTHA: You mean divine intercourse, don't you? (*laughs, surprised at her play on the word*) When I lock your hams between my legs and anchor my meathooks in your back, your eyes will bug out like hardboiled eggs! Your tongue will scream for mercy! You won't be reciting no Jack somebody! You won't be playing no Beethoven with your toes! You'll wish you was back on some goatskin bed in the middle of darkest Africa with your two black brides and one of them lizards! You'll see whose breasts can jiggle fur like it was silk!

EDDIE (*to PRIEST*): Which capital sin might be the root of such pornographic pyrotechnics?

BERTHA (*comes out door USL with armful of dirty towels*): You writers and all them big words. If you aint a funny...Father!

23

PRIEST: Bertha, my dear. I'm sorry...

BERTHA: Mr. Jones...

EDDIE: Think nothing of it, dear...

PRIEST: I had no idea. I thought Mr. Jones was alone...

EDDIE: We will pray for your salvation, Bertha. Or are
  you Lutheran?

BERTHA: Mr. Jones, don't you forget to swallow them
  pills!

> (BERTHA exits French doors and Stretch cart
> quickly offstage USL.)

PRIEST: You seem in lively spirits.

EDDIE (*picks up one paper cup from tray table*): And you
  seem Pastor O'Malley of half-lace-curtain Irish.

PRIEST: But I am Irish.

EDDIE: You can't help it I guess. Any more than I can help
  it I don't have the black ass, Padre. I'm pretty beat up but
  I think I'm going to beat this joint.

PRIEST: Doctor Drake told me you've become quite
  docile.

EDDIE: Limp from toenails to tips of graying hairs, not to
  mention withering genitals.

PRIEST: Somehow I feel you are not docile at all.

EDDIE (*walks through door to bathroom USR and yells*):
If medicos want docile I can run as a docile. Don't need
brain all fogged over. Been directing horse pills south
via Mississippi via can. Gulf of Mexico now full of
compliant fish. (*toilet flushes*) Bon voyage!

PRIEST: God bless you anyway.

EDDIE (*emerges from bathroom*): How is the old gent? I'd
like to meet him some day.

PRIEST: You shall see his light. But outside time...

EDDIE: He helped Andrea del Sarto paint girl in the Prado
I've loved the longest. (*to Shakespeare*) Except for forty
paragraphs he edited Huck Finn. (*to PRIEST*) He fought
for both sides at Gettysburg. He designed my aluminum
kneecap and knocked yellow fever on its ass. He sired
and foaled Citation. But I never met the old gent.

PRIEST: You shall.

EDDIE: Ecclesiastes wasn't as sure...

PRIEST: Read his inspired words again, Eddie. Chapter
twelve, verses nine to fourteen.

EDDIE: Tacked on. By overzealous monk on a slow day.

PRIEST: Eddie, pray with me. Let his light in.

EDDIE: Pray! In first so-called world war, I was plenty
scared after I got wounded. Very devout then. Feared
death. Needed personal salvation. So I did pray for
meddling from polyglot of saints...

PRIEST: You see...

EDDIE: Prayed with tribal faith. Spanish civil war ended that. Selfish to pray for my behalf when all people all sides suffered very bad things.

PRIEST: Chaos is all the more reason to pray for light.

EDDIE: I miss praying for myself! Miss ghostly comfort the way a man who runs as a drinker but not a rummy misses his drink when he is wet and very cold.

PRIEST: The holy spirit is tugging on you...

EDDIE: Last war - don't mean Korea, only goddamned one I missed - I got through without praying once. Times bad too.

PRIEST: The entire second world war without a prayer!

EDDIE: I forfeited my right to pray. It was absolutely crooked to ask for help no matter how scared I was.

PRIEST: But that's the beauty of our faith. Jesus always forgives.

EDDIE: That guy...

PRIEST: Eddie, you're tangled up in the old covenant.

EDDIE: Even that old stuff runs twenty-seven shades of gray. How do you know I'm not stuck in earliest Ecclesiastes which is about as comforting as looking at your own embalmed face in your own coffin. But admit I was almost sucker for that new covenant once.

PRIEST: Eddie, pray with me.

EDDIE: He was tough in there...

PRIEST: No one was ever tougher than Jesus Christ.

EDDIE: ...for a while.

PRIEST: Courage under pressure.

EDDIE: I thought that once too.

PRIEST: Once?

EDDIE: He didn't measure up. Padre, he yellowed out!

PRIEST: Yellow!

EDDIE: Christ yellowed out on the cross...

PRIEST: All that pain! Suffering! How can you say that?

EDDIE: Horse's mouth! Saint Mark, chapter fifteen, verse thirty-four: And at the ninth hour, Jesus cried with a loud voice, saying, Eloi, Eloi, lama sabachthani? which is, in King James English, My God, my God, why hast thou forsaken me?

PRIEST: Is that why you...

EDDIE: Makes whole thing crooked.

PRIEST: Eddie, he fulfilled prophecy of Psalm twenty-two, verse one: My God, my God, why hast thou forsaken me?

EDDIE: Picked goddamned bad time to quote David.

PRIEST: Don't forget, like all our Lord's painfully truthful followers, Mark added 'And some of them that stood by, when they heard it, said, Behold, he calleth Elias.'

EDDIE: Matthew twenty-seven, forty-six: And about the ninth hour, Jesus cried with a loud voice....

PRIEST (*so agitated he interrupts*): The next verse says: Some of them that stood there, when they heard that, said, This man calleth for Elias. And, Eddie, Saint John doesn't mention it at all, nor did Saint Luke...

EDDIE: If it hadn't been Mark. (*to Shakespeare*) Mark too simple-minded to make it up.

PRIEST: You recite passages perfectly...

EDDIE (*fiery*): Good writer has got to know as much as he can of everything. Has to be born with ability to learn quicker than other men. Has to reject as bullshit or accept as true gen what is already presented as knowledge. He can not learn everything quickly though and time, (*to Shakespeare in depressed voice*) which is all he has got, is paid dearly to acquire some things. They are the simplest things of all and because it takes a lifetime to learn them the little new that he gets from life is very costly...but the only heritage he has to leave.

PRIEST: But you really know holy scripture.

EDDIE: Good place to dig for titles. Especially Ecclesiastes.

PRIEST: Eddie, titles?

EDDIE: One generation passeth away, and another
   generation cometh: but the earth abideth forever. The
   sun also ariseth, and the sun goeth down, and hasteth to
   the place where he arose...about six titles there.

PRIEST: Just titles?

EDDIE: I returned, and saw under the sun, that the race is
   not to the swift, nor the battle to the strong, neither yet
   bread to the wise, nor yet riches to men of
   understanding, nor yet favor to men of skill; but time
   and chance happeneth to them all...

PRIEST (*gently*): Titles...

EDDIE (*wistfully to Shakespeare*): So goddamned true it's
   truer than life itself, like the best writing...

PRIEST: Eddie, are you all right?

EDDIE: So goddamned beautiful in its truth and so
   goddamned cosmically cruel I could cry.

PRIEST: Edward Hathaway cry?

EDDIE: I'm Mr. Jones, remember? Anyway, I'm not talking
   about crybabyismo, which is just running as a whiner.

PRIEST: But really crying?

EDDIE: When the hurt is bad enough, I cry.

PRIEST: Like Christ on the cross. You can't fool me about Jesus. You came back to our Lord in your old man in the boat story. The light was too strong...

EDDIE (*embarrassed enough to sound pompous*): I moved on past calculus with that one. Nobody in history or myth shows any better than Christ how this nutty world grinds up a good man and destroys him. But if the man doesn't yellow out...the world can never defeat him, just destroy him.

PRIEST: Eddie, you are Christian.

EDDIE: Can't imagine taking another religion seriously. Padre, that endorsement too strong?

PRIEST: And you are Catholic too.

EDDIE: Second marriage did that. Was impotent from 'I do', got desperate enough to drink calf's blood as if that might pump it up. Didn't work. Against my own wisdom I let new wife talk me into ancient superstition. Went to small church at dawn and said small prayer for flacid member. Came back with a spike and we didn't uncouple for three days and two nights. Got rid of wife but member has been Catholic ever since.

PRIEST: I will pray for you.

EDDIE: Well, if you're running that goddamned far gone, I'll pray for you. Can't guarantee divine intervention.

PRIEST: So it's not yellow to pray for me.

EDDIE: In spades.

PRIEST: Why are you fooling the doctor?

EDDIE: He's killing my memory. It's my capital. It's all I have left. It's my center. It's my legacy.

PRIEST: That's sad. Like putting out candles. Killing memory.

EDDIE: Goddamn it all, couldn't remember Irati River this morning. (*to Shakespeare*) Put almost a whole goddamn book there.

PRIEST: That's very sad, Eddie. Like a cloudy day. But you just quoted entire passages from the bible.

EDDIE: Reference section okay. My own stuff checked out a lot of the time.

PRIEST: Take your medication.

EDDIE: If I took every goddamned pill they gave me you could close the library and put me in a salad.

PRIEST (*walking to window*): That's very sad.

EDDIE: Goddamn drugs give me black ass and make it worse. Everything checked out. Goddamn pills will burn up my whole library...

PRIEST: It's dark in here. (*starts to open the drapes*) Let the doctor help you. Let me pray for you. For a while.

EDDIE: They did it to me again yesterday. I heard that's the last one. I've got to clear out of this joint!

(PRIEST opens drapes suddenly. The window is barred!)

PRIEST: Eddie, they say you might be confused enough to give up hope...

(EDDIE walks stiffly US to wall between bed and bathroom door and pretends to look at his papers on the wall.)

EDDIE: Suicide! Say it! Goddamn it anyway, that's my business.

PRIEST: They can't let you out if they think you're suicidal.

EDDIE: Is that why you're nosing around?

PRIEST: I thought we were friends.

EDDIE: Sorry. Goddamn it, that just proves the drugs are still in me.

PRIEST: Eddie, you're going to be in his light again.

EDDIE: Used to wait ten years between books (*to Shakespeare*) but I had knowledge solid inside me I could still write.

PRIEST: You can still...

EDDIE: One day without knowledge of working good again is eternity. Never think that black-ass way except on goddamned pills.

PRIEST (*doubtfully*): The medication must help you...

EDDIE: Get the words right? Stay healthy? Eat and drink with friends? Enjoy myself in bed?

PRIEST: Yes.

EDDIE: Do you know how many of those things I have when I take the pills? None!

PRIEST (*cautiously*): How about the Feds?

EDDIE: Feds?

PRIEST: Are the Feds still following you?

EDDIE: Padre, that was a delusion. I'm all over that. Momentary imaging of overheated imagination. My built-in shock-resistant bullshit detector is running okay again.

PRIEST: Thank God for that, Eddie. I'll pray for you.

EDDIE: I'll pray for you.

PRIEST: Suicide is never the answer. It's...it's yellow.

EDDIE: Yellow?

PRIEST: Coward's way out. Yellow. Very yellow.

EDDIE: Yellow? Look down the bore of a five oh five Gibbs which can drop ten thousand pounds of elephant faster than God can and think what that Gibbs will do to your melon-sized head if your finger can just squeeze the trigger which is harder to budge than the last goddamn turn of the key on a sardine can!

PRIEST: Please to God, no. Think of your writing, Eddie. Think of recovery. I'll be back, Eddie. I'll pray for brighter days. It's okay for me to pray for you.

EDDIE: Yeah...

(PRIEST goes out French doors, feels head with a shudder, walks tightly to exit USL.)

Think of my writing! (*to Shakespeare*) Goddamn, the lack of it is all I ever think of when I'm riding those narcotics. I'll live on my terms. Or... (*walks over quickly to pull drapes shut, then peek out*) Sonuvabitch! (*jumps away from window and hugs the wall*) That was close! Feds are all over the parking lot thicker than ticks on a baboon's prick.

End of Act One

ACT TWO

Drake's office. Stage left is an oblique wall with open French doors USL. Drapes are open on an unbarred window on the US wall. In middle of US wall hangs a picture of Sigmund Freud. On SR wall of the room stands a large open cabinet USR. A human skeleton dangles inside the cabinet. DSR on the same wall is an enormous labeled diagram of the human brain. SC, a chair and a desk face left. On the desk are a black dial phone and a large-mouth glass bottle with a pickled brain. L.C. sits in one of two chairs SL that face the desk. He is writing in his notebook. MAGGIE stands by the cabinet and stares morbidly at the skeleton.

MAGGIE: Eddie looks terrible, doesn't he?

L.C. (*not looking up*): The weight loss. A temporary downtick...

MAGGIE: His face seems undefined...

L.C.: Pops seemed stable.

MAGGIE: They are trying to drop his cholesterol from four hundred something to just a little over two hundred.

L.C.: He was combative, yet civil. Like a...a good Wall Street lawyer.

MAGGIE: His blood pressure may be getting better.

L.C. (*looking over the office and jotting notes*): I saw all his readings on the wall. He was lucid.

MAGGIE: L.C., you're not thinking about writing about all this, are you?

L.C.: Are you referring to the notes I take? It's just habit. I'm a writer.

MAGGIE: I'm a writer too. But I'm not thinking about a book. I'm thinking about Eddie.

L.C.: So am I. You can refer to my notes anytime. It's a habit. And a necessity. I don't have a mind like Eddie, who never had to take notes.

MAGGIE: No book?

L.C.: (*evasively*) Nothing planned. Sorry if my note-taking is a bother.

MAGGIE: I'll try to ignore it. Just so it's not for a book. Let's get back to Eddie. They cut him back to just two glasses of wine at dinner.

L.C.: He was focused. Like a...a good banker. (*staring at desk*) My God, that's a real brain!

MAGGIE: L.C., Eddie's a wreck!

L.C.: Maggie!

MAGGIE: He's so clever. (*sits down and leans toward L.C.*) Crazy with me, then shrewd as an old wounded buffalo bull around everybody else. I was hoping...

L.C.: He would snap.

MAGGIE: Yes.

L.C.: For you, you needled him pretty good.

MAGGIE: He hasn't improved.

L.C. (*doubtfully and reluctant to stop writing notes*): Still deluded?

(DRAKE walks onstage USR and stops outside the French doors.)

MAGGIE: More than ever.

L.C.: But didn't you say they've given him a complete series...

(DRAKE strides breezily into office.)

DRAKE: Mr. Hathaway looks and sounds like a Seth Thomas, doesn't he? (*enthused*) Yes, the old clock has been refurbished...(*notices L.C. taking notes and frowns*)

MAGGIE (*very stiff*): I wish to discuss the possibility of his release.

DRAKE: His release is precisely what we all want.

MAGGIE: I'm not advocating his release! Not until I see some positive...

DRAKE: That's what the clinic is here for. Weigh positives, weigh negatives. And not just numbers and graphs, but qualitative feelings of people who tend to Edward Hathaway. Not just me, but even his nurses. Nurse Grace says he is as relaxed as any old gentleman she's cared for. Even Bertha gets along with him. Weight is even given to his babbles with the priest. The priest jabbers to him all the time. How about you, Mr. Rankin? Have you formed an opinion?

L.C.: The name is Mankin. I would like to talk to all those people you just mentioned...

DRAKE: Not necessary. I have interviewed each and every one carefully, recording copious notes and assigning proper weights.

L.C.: Seems like Mrs. Hathaway and I should have an accounting from them.

DRAKE: I understand your concern but it is not necessary.

L.C.: Seems like we should audit the books, so to speak.

DRAKE: Are you serious?

MAGGIE: We should!

DRAKE: They are all working now, even the priest in a sense.

MAGGIE: Can't you page them?

L.C.: Seems like we should talk to them.

(After awkward silence of ten seconds, DRAKE picks up the phone and dials four numbers.)

DRAKE: Nurse Grace? Uh, not now...no, not now I said! Would you please send Father to my office? And you better stick around yourself.

L.C.: And nurse Bertha...

DRAKE: Bertha?

L.C.: You mentioned a nurse Bertha.

DRAKE: I did?

MAGGIE: Yes, you did.

DRAKE (*disgusted*): And round up nurse Bertha too. Yes, I said Bertha! (*slams down phone*) Frankly, although Bertha is quite adequate as a nurse, she knows nothing of psychiatry.

MAGGIE: I would not expect her to know anything more than symptoms. I don't.

DRAKE: A complex man like Mr. Hathaway might confuse someone simple. Like Bertha.

MAGGIE: If you're thinking of releasing Eddie, doctor, then he has confused you too.

DRAKE: Let's not prejudge.

(GRACE prances outside French doors USL.)

L.C. (*agreeably*): Pops did look solid as a war bond except for the weight.

MAGGIE: My God, I hope he didn't fool you too.

DRAKE: Mrs. Hathaway, you're too close. You hear a squeak in the lid of the glove box but the engine is running fine.

L.C.: No one who knows Maggie would ever discredit for one second her deep concern, her unflagging devotion to Pops.

MAGGIE: You must not release Eddie. I just couldn't handle...

(GRACE raps on the doorway.)

DRAKE: Perhaps you could put your notebook away, Mr. Rankin. We promised Edward Hathaway complete confidentiality. (*waits as L.C. frowns and puts his notebook in his inside coat pocket*) Come in, please.

GRACE (*walks in until she is one step from DRAKE*): You wanted me, doctor?

DRAKE (*rises to walk over by the cabinet USR*): We have a question about Edward Hath...Edward Jones. Do you think Mr. Jones acts deluded in any way?

MAGGIE: With and without medication! And who will guarantee he takes it?

DRAKE (*angry*): Maybe the nurse could just tell us her general impression of Mr. Jones, without qualifications.

GRACE: Mr. Jones is always such an old gentleman. I could just hug him. So relaxed...

MAGGIE: When drugged. Did he mention anything about the Feds?

GRACE: Feds? (*looks at DRAKE*) No. Not for a long time.

(PRIEST comes onstage USR and stops outside the French doors.)

DRAKE: Thank you, nurse.

L.C.: Nurse, does he talk about anybody else?

GRACE: He's just real relaxed. Just cozies into that chair. No problem at all. He just drones on. All talk. Not like some of the men...

DRAKE: That's enough, nurse. (*sees PRIEST standing in doorway*) Father! Come in. Thank you, nurse.

L.C.: Be sure and send nurse Bertha.

GRACE (*looking at DRAKE*): I couldn't find her. Do you really want me to keep groping around for Bertha?

DRAKE (*dejected*): Of course.

(GRACE flounces from the room to exit USL. DRAKE walks over and stands by picture of Freud. PRIEST enters tentatively.)

Father, we were discussing Edward Jones.

PRIEST: Jones? Oh, of course, Mr. Jones...

MAGGIE: And the foolhardiness of his release.

DRAKE: Father, would you say Mr. Jones is Roman Catholic?

PRIEST: He certainly professes that...

MAGGIE: Father...

PRIEST: In his own contrary way.

MAGGIE: Don't you see what he's getting at?

L.C.: Yes. How sure are you?

PRIEST: He does profess to be Catholic.

DRAKE: Is Edward Jones rational?

PRIEST: He seemed rational when I last talked to him. No more than half an hour ago.

MAGGIE: Did he peek out the drapes while you talked to him?

L.C.: Yes, did he?

PRIEST: As of matter of fact, I opened the curtains.

MAGGIE: You did?

DRAKE: You see!

(BERTHA comes onstage USL. Although her hands are balled into fists, she approaches the doorway hesitantly.)

MAGGIE: Do you think he could stand the drapes open if he were undrugged?

PRIEST: Truthfully I would have to say yes. I'm not so sure about his release though...

DRAKE: His release is not your call to make, Father. Thank you.

(BERTHA raps softly.)

L.C.: I'd like to get into...

(BERTHA steps in tentatively. When she sees PRIEST, she becomes very nervous.)

PRIEST: Bertha, my dear.

DRAKE: Come in, nurse. Thank you, Father.

PRIEST: I'm not so sure...

MAGGIE: Father, stay.

DRAKE: I think you understand, Mrs. Hath...Mrs. Jones. We can't discuss this now. Thank you, Father.

PRIEST: It seems unfinished. Is it possible he's most dangerous to himself when he IS medicated? What if the center of his being works only in his delusion now? What if...

> (DRAKE takes PRIEST by arm to coax him out the door)

DRAKE: I agree it's unfinished, Father. Thank you so much for your theological observations. Bertha, we are discussing Mr. Jones.

L.C.: Yes, we'd like your impression of his stability.

MAGGIE: Drugged and undrugged.

> (PRIEST exits reluctantly USR, shaking his head in exasperation. DRAKE sits on the edge of his desk, fondling the bottle.)

DRAKE: I see no reason for everyone to hypothesize on his undrugged state.

BERTHA: Undrugged? (*relieved she is not going to be reprimanded because of what the PRIEST overheard earlier*) He would be just as calm as a cucumber undrugged...(*looks at DRAKE*) probably.

DRAKE: Oh? Thank you, nurse...

L.C.: Undrugged?

MAGGIE: Are you sure?

BERTHA (*feeling better every second*): He aint no ordinary fare, I can tell you that.

DRAKE: I can't see how this speculation is helping at all.

L.C.: But she seems to be on the same currency as Pops.

MAGGIE: Do you really think he would be all right undrugged?

BERTHA: Writers are a funny bunch of eggs but Mr. Jones is ready as watermelon in September... (*looks at DRAKE*) probably.

DRAKE: Well, we won't try to quantify that. Thank you, nurse.

(BERTHA spins to leave the room and exit USL.)

Bertha believes he would be relaxed even unmedicated, so in a sense she was helpful. (*amazed*) Actually helpful.

MAGGIE: I'd give everything I have to make sure she was right.

DRAKE: Bertha confirmed what the professional staff already know. Not to mention the priest's confirmation, which is quite important to a possibility some of us might have weighing on our minds. But I have more good news for you. Why don't I run through the medical results now?

L.C. (*pulling out his notebook*): We need to discuss every asset, every deficit.

DRAKE: Mr. Rankin, may I remind of confidentiality.

L.C.: (*putting away his notebook*) Sorry. Habit.

45

MAGGIE: Somehow I have a feeling this is going to be a nice long list of attributes with nice safe numbers...

DRAKE: Mrs. Hathaway, science does try to quantify. Otherwise, we would just be in the Dark Ages, waving our arms like that priest, invoking supernatural powers to heal.

L.C.: Maybe we could get into your balance sheet...

MAGGIE: Nowhere in that list will be a number that tells what Eddie will do next.

DRAKE: And nowhere in the list will there be a number that specifies a man should be free. Or a man should be incarcerated. Mrs. Hathaway, I am not a jailor.

L.C.: Maybe we should just get into your evaluation.

MAGGIE (*very depressed*): Go ahead.

DRAKE: Thank you.

L.C.: It would help me if you could describe the underlying liability.

DRAKE: Apparently, over the years Edward Hathaway sustained (*hesitates as L.C. scribbles with his finger on his thigh*) a head injury or two.

MAGGIE: Or twenty!

L.C.: God yes. Even before the plane crashes. God yes. Horrid head injury on his boat in nineteen fifty-one. Five during the second war. Bloody one in Paris before that.

Not to mention the mortar, that minenwerfer full of bolts and nuts and scraps of metal that blew off his kneecap in the first war. That would bankrupt any man's soul.

MAGGIE: Not to mention his drinking.

L.C.: God yes. He made a run once of sixteen double daiquiris at La Floridita.

DRAKE: He has voluntarily subdued his drinking and I can't heal a soul, whatever that is. Anyway, it's definite these head traumas did accumulate enough stress to cause deep anxieties - worries about returning to the poverty he once endured - worries about losing his stature as a writer, which is big enough now to make any man worry.

L.C.: He suffered more loss than stress and anxiety.

MAGGIE: Suffered? Someone said he was manic depressive...

DRAKE: Please, Mrs. Hathaway, that requires psychiatric determination.

MAGGIE: But he's highly active for days, either working, bullying somebody or talking. If only you could hear him drone for hours on end. Then he's low for days, drinking and still talking.

DRAKE: A layman's observation. But many think Teddy Roosevelt was manic depressive. He certainly functioned all right.

MAGGIE (*numb*): That's his hero. Eddie even had to have the same white hunter in Africa that Teddy Roosevelt had so many years earlier. Not once but twice. First in the nineteen thirties, then the last time with me in the early nineteen fifties. The old hunter was practically in a wheelchair.

DRAKE: Let me get on with facts. Edward Hathaway began to show symptoms of obsession because of the stress. He could rationalize his obsessions and overcome them. But the stress increased until delusions began. These he could not rationalize. He believed the delusions with all his...(*bothered by L.C. constantly scribbling with his finger on his thigh*) his intellect. He drifted back and forth between obsession, which he could master, and delusion, which he could not master.

L.C.: Prior to his treatments.

MAGGIE: He still swings back and forth. That's him exactly.

DRAKE: I insist categorically the delusions have disappeared since he's had a full series of ECTs.

L.C.: Translate, doctor.

MAGGIE: And he needs more shock treatments...

DRAKE: Electro Convulsive Treatments.

L.C.: Shock treatments. Poor Pops.

DRAKE: It's not the nightmare of a lie you've seen in moving pictures, Mr. Rankin. We don't strap a patient down and electrocute him. We tranquilize him and while he is sedated we administer the treatment. The patient remembers absolutely nothing.

L.C.: Poor Pops.

MAGGIE: He needs them!

DRAKE: Edward Hathaway had the full series of eleven. I have to admit we don't understand exactly what happens to a patient in ECT but it does wonders for a patient and it has unequivocally done wonders for Mr. Hathaway. Oh, he complains about loss of memory. He's slightly confused. But those are standard side effects. He has no memory of the treatment, yet over several months he will recover all memories prior to treatment. What could be nicer than that?

MAGGIE (*obviously reciting something memorized*): Psychological help can't even begin until the electrical shocks neutralize... (*looks at DRAKE for help*)

DRAKE: ...the psychopathological symptoms. I insist we have neutralized them with Electro Convulsive Treatments. And, Mrs. Hathaway, please, we do not use the term shock.

L.C.: Psychological treatment has not begun?

MAGGIE: No. And he needs more shock...

DRAKE: Psychological treatment is well underway. Edward Hathaway is two-thirds restored. Medication stabilizes him. He may have an obsessive thought now and then but he can deal with obsessions. He no longer has delusions.

L.C.: Pops is no normal commodity. Are you sure he might not still have delusions because his delusions are more resistant, more...

MAGGIE: Yes! That's it exactly!

DRAKE: You've answered it yourself. If Edward Hathaway is half again a normal man, then two-thirds of that puts him right back in the norm, doesn't it?

L.C.: I'm not sure that adds up...

MAGGIE: He needs more...

DRAKE: Let me sum up. Edward Hathaway is immensely improved. He swims every day. He diets rigorously. He drinks only a glass or two of wine with dinner. I've had him dine at my house. He's a charming guest. My wife says he knows more stories than Scheherazade. One of the doctors took him skeet shooting. Mr. Hathaway is cantankerous but steady as a surgeon. Best of all, he is making a determined mental effort. In fact, he loaned me the book he just finished. (*opens desk drawer and pulls out a book*) Here it is. Margins are full of notes too.

L.C. (*ignoring the book*): God knows I hate to see Pops locked up, out of circulation.

DRAKE: He is not locked up here. We are not that kind of institution. Truth is, he can leave anytime he wants.

L.C.: But you can use persuasion.

MAGGIE: Yes!

DRAKE: Mr. Rankin, what is your opinion?

L.C.: Mankin. (*hesitates*) Maggie, I don't see how I can dispute the total assessment. Even the priest and that nurse Bertha think...

MAGGIE (*jumps up*): You are going to release him! Good lord, what am I going to do? L.C., you must talk to him again! You must!

DRAKE: I will prepare the papers for his release.

L.C.: Maggie, I wish...

MAGGIE: I'm going to the hotel!

(MAGGIE dashes through the French doors and runs offstage USL. L.C. reluctantly stands up to follow her.)

DRAKE: Mrs. Hathaway! (*to L.C.*) You better go after her.

L.C.: No. I want to talk to Pops. In this room. Alone.

DRAKE: Of course you can talk to him. (*picks up phone and dials four numbers*) Nurse? No, not now...nurse, bring Mr. Jones to my office. (*hangs up and feels his inside coat pocket*)

L.C.: The papers are already made out, aren't they?

DRAKE: Mr. Jones...Hathaway will be here shortly. You'll be convinced.

(DRAKE walks out and exits USL.)

L.C. (*pulls out notebook to scribble frantically*): He already had the papers made out. (*leaps up*) I better go after Maggie. Even if I don't catch up to her.

(Still scribbling and glancing at his wristwatch L.C. exits slowly through the French doors and saunters offstage USL, absorbed in his scribbling.)

(Within seconds GRACE appears USL, followed by EDDIE. She carries a blanket. He wears a oversized white guayabera, baggy tweed pants and moccasins. He clutches something dark in both hands. When they reach the French doors, he sees that no one awaits them and strides boldly into the office.)

GRACE (*by chair*): Mr. Jones, sit down here.

EDDIE: In a goddamn minute.

GRACE: Now! I won't take my paws off you until you sit down.

EDDIE (*sits down*): My mind is udderly awash with milk-swollen protuberances.

GRACE (*bends over and tucks blanket over his lap*): Whatever that means. There, there, Mr. Jones. You just nuzzle your rear into that chair and relax now.

EDDIE: Tuck that goddamn thing and leave. We are moving into ten-dollar stakes and you dropped out on penny ante.

GRACE (*still bent over, groping in his crotch*): Whatever that means. Mr. Jones, you are always such a fine old gentleman. (*puzzled*) So relax... (*stands up abruptly*) Are you sure you took those pills?

EDDIE: Affirmed. Think of no pills taken and shudder. Goddamn, start with a sick woman and see where you get. Sick in the head or sick anywhere. But sick anywhere and in a little while they're sick in the head. Nasty as hell. Too bovinely stupid to know hardon was the shiv.

GRACE (*hands on hips, agitated enough to turn ugly*): Mr. Jones, your combover is off the mark today.

EDDIE (*surprised*): Once wrote 'Never trust a man who slicks hair over a bald head'.

GRACE (*pleased*): And your red mask of psoriasis is flaking all over.

EDDIE: Good thing shirt is white. Once satirized reptilian skin of Sinclair Lewis.

GRACE: Your balding and your rotting skin don't bother me, Mr. Jones. Not even your bloody urine or edema.

EDDIE: That's about as heartwarming as a letter of recommendation from a Nairobi whorehouse.

GRACE: But I better tell you what bothers me most before you dry up and blow away. Somebody said you used to weigh over 200. What do you weigh now? 150?

EDDIE: (*lifelessly*): 155.

GRACE: Mr. Jones, what bothers me is your stench. You and your phony alcohol bathes. You reek of sweat, urine and excrement. I've heard of your type. You have power over people, so you double your sick pleasure by making them smell your shit.

EDDIE (*impressed*): A mind behind those glands? A real bitch with handles too. I should irrigate you.

GRACE (*smoothing dress to emphasize bust*): Whatever that means. Don't forget to consult that plaster head on your desk, Einstein.

> (GRACE ignores him angrily but finally leaves the room and exits USR. As EDDIE sees L.C. enter USL he slaps the skullcap on his head, immediately rises and flings the blanket against the wall USC. He bounces on the balls of his feet like a boxer but his arms hang limp. Now he throws a left jab)

L.C. (*coming through the French doors and hastily putting away his notebook*): Pops!

EDDIE: By Christ, L.C., I feel like we just put four lines out in the dark-blue water of the Gulf Stream.

L.C.: By God, Pops. You're full of zip! You look like you just sniffed out Man O War at twenty to one...

EDDIE: (*shakes hands with his left arm slapping L.C.'s back*): Do I detect an old pal losing confidence in the firm? It's that goddamn room. Goddamn bars...

L.C.: Any winner would be diminished by that.

EDDIE: That room would give any man the black ass.

L.C.: By God, I feel better seeing you like this. You just became the prohibitive favorite again.

EDDIE (*still bouncing, starts sparring with the skeleton*): Goddamn right! This is Kid Hathaway. Remember? I took out old Chekhov (*hammers a roundhouse right*) and Marvell (*a roundhouse left*) and even Jack Donne (*dandy combination*) and the good Kipling (*left jab*) and Thoreau (*right uppercut*) and Dante (*left hook*) and Virgil (*right hook*) - almost at opening bell.

L.C.: By God yes, Pops. You did.

EDDIE: Mark Twain wrote one good book and one mountain of hog wash.

L.C.: Sure, Pops. You took him out a long time ago. Several times over.

EDDIE (*bounces over to picture of Freud*): So I moved up and nailed Turgenev in two (*combination*), DeMaupassant in three (*finishes him with an uppercut*), Stendahl in four (*left jab and right cross*), Flaubert in five (*mad flurry of punches*). Frogs fractured and scattered everywhere!

L.C.: Bravo!

EDDIE (*bouncing on his feet back to skeleton*): Shit-maru! L.C., you know I can't stop. I've got Mr. Cervantes on the card. Might have to go twenty.

L.C.: You'll put him away in eight.

EDDIE: Then Melville.

L.C.: Whale of a fight. You harpoon him in ten.

EDDIE (*sparring*): Dostoevsky. Goddamn. He never got the words right. How can a man write so unbelievably badly and make you feel so deeply? You read him and his stuff is so true it changes your life. Made me rethink whole goddamn machinery. Have to train hard for him, L.C. Very hard.

L.C.: You can take him, Pops. Maybe you have to coast the middle rounds. Like you are coasting now! In this place, Pops. You're just coasting. So you can take him out in the twelfth. No later than fifteen.

EDDIE: Then twenty rounds with Ten Ton Tolstoy. (*suddenly tired*) By Christ though, on my very best day he might knock my ears off.

L.C.: Never say quit, Pops. Nobody knocked you down yet.

EDDIE (*sparring but very tired*): Never get to old Bill Shakespeare. No need. Nobody can lay a glove on his snoot anyway. He's up there on Olympus, L.C. Maybe beyond.

L.C.: Forget Shakespeare. You can't train too far ahead. You've got Cervantes to think about. Continue working with your notes on Paris you found in the basement of the Ritz, Pops. Work them up into the truest story yet on the lost generation.

EDDIE: Lost! That goddamned Gertrude Stein. (*touches L.C.'s shoulder apologetically*) I'm a little pooped.

L.C.: You are pooped but undefeated.

EDDIE: Undefeated but pooped.

L.C.: The old double dicho. Pure as the heart of a champion.

EDDIE: Man can be destroyed but never defeated.

L.C.: Man can be defeated but never destroyed.

EDDIE: Best goddamn double dicho ever.

L.C.: By God, Pops. You really look terrific. You really have the firm back in shape.

EDDIE: Dropped from full-fledged heavyweight to half-assed middleweight but certainly don't have dire crud the medicos here talk about. I'm a little beat up but not in the clutch. (*stares at window for ten seconds and strolls away from it to USL*) Listen, L.C., I'm plenty worried about Miss Maggie...

L.C.: Maggie?

EDDIE: She's been running as a straight sad.

L.C.: Maggie is just worried about you.

EDDIE: Thought I was the one hurt when those goddamned kites kept falling out of the sky over Africa. (*points at head*) I don't mean to sound like a morbid but Miss Maggie got beat up too.

L.C.: Maggie? I didn't know.

EDDIE: Nobody but me knows how much. Shit-maru, I feel like I'm pissing in my father's beer...

L.C.: Maggie?

EDDIE: L.C., she's running pretty sick.

L.C.: She seemed all right to me.

EDDIE: You don't see how she works me like a goddamned picador?

L.C.: Picador?

EDDIE: Picking and picking and picking. In my neck and both shoulders, L.C. Blood crusted down to my ankles. Layer upon goddamned layer of blood.

L.C.: Maybe she just wants to arouse your faculties...

EDDIE: To act? Can't pull Willie Blake opposition is true friendship bullshit out for this one. Miss Maggie's running as a crazy.

L.C. (*dejected*): Crazy? All right, Pops. Let's talk about what we should do about it.

EDDIE: Goddamn, it's good to have somebody sane to talk to. I have nobody here.

L.C.: Let's talk.

EDDIE: The true gen is Maggie wants to keep me here.

L.C.: It's not like that exactly.

EDDIE: She's got her eye on some goddamned ski bum in Sun Valley.

L.C.: Pops...

EDDIE: I know it doesn't sound like the true gen.

L.C.: She loves you.

EDDIE: Loves my royalties.

L.C.: Pops... (*picks up book*) I hear you're reading again.

EDDIE: Ever read that bird?

L.C.: My God.

EDDIE: Ever read him?

L.C.: You read this book two years ago.

EDDIE: I read books again and again. Huck Finn about ten times. Even a club fighter can get in a lucky punch. But what a lucky punch. Best book any American ever wrote. Like to fix about forty paragraphs though...

L.C.: You even wrote a puff for this dust jacket.

EDDIE: Got the words right too.

L.C.: And the doctor thinks you are reading again...

EDDIE (*now stands by side of window, looking out cautiously*): Sonuvabitch! Couple of J. Edgars...

L.C.: Who?

EDDIE: I thought you said my lawyer reported that goddamned bet.

L.C.: What bet?

EDDIE: Shit-maru! You don't even remember what I'm talking about. The goddamned four Gs I won on the Swede.

L.C.: That was two years ago, Pops. Almost to the day.

EDDIE: And I was worried about those goddamned European royalties going to Switzerland.

L.C.: Pops. Your taxes are all right.

EDDIE: My eyes tell the firm otherwise. Two kinds of jerks I spot easy as Eskimos at Wimbledon...

L.C.: Pops, Maggie is your best...

EDDIE: Bull dykes in tweed suits and low cut oxfords. Pompadour hair and tendency to scream like hell in your face...

L.C.: Maggie is your...

EDDIE: And those jerks! Dark suits, white shirts, cuff links...

L.C. (*now looking out the window too*): They're carrying medical bags.

EDDIE: What the goddamned hell did you think they tote in here? Violin cases? Not even J. Edgars are that dumb. Look at the burrheads reflect the sun. Sonuvabitch. (*closes drapes violently*) Maybe it's the Italian girl I had brought to New York. That is it! Goddamn it. I didn't even get to see her, let alone deflower her. Just paid for her goddamned ticket. Sixteen years old. The jerks would follow you to the ends of the earth to prosecute you for impairing the morals of a minor.

L.C.: Pops...

EDDIE: I was okay as long as Eleanor could keep Franco's Bastard Irish off my back. Goddamn, now she's running as global aristocrat and she hears practically nothing that is said to her but she's so charming people don't notice...

L.C.: Pops...

EDDIE: Prez was sexless, like a great lumpy woman Secretary of Labor. Sure can't intercede from the worm circus where he presides.

L.C.: Pops...

61

EDDIE: You think this is easy on me? Now Miss Maggie can't ever go back to New York. They'll nail me for impairing the morals of a minor. Or a hundred other things all my so-called pals stooled on me.

L.C.: Pops...

EDDIE: Can't go back to Idaho. Maggie's carrying on there. Ski bum found out she is most enthused fornicator on planet. He is probably bushwhacker. Get me from behind. Right in the back of my head which has been hurt already about a hundred times. And state jerks are after me for taxes anyway.

L.C.: Stay here, Pops. It's secure here. Safe as Fort Knox.

EDDIE: I'm caged here. I can't exist on these terms.

L.C.: Don't talk that way. You never scratched a race yet!

EDDIE (*standing at desk, looking at the pickled brain*): You'd like me to stay here! Like a goddamned hothouse tomato. You come around once in a while and pump me for my Paris stories while I butt brains with the Karamazovs and then you go out and pedal them. Edward Hathaway's devoted liaison with world. Lucrative intermediary for reclusive vegetable Hathaway, (*salutes bottle*) who ends up pickled in a goddamned bottle.

L.C.: Pops, you asked me to look after your work.

EDDIE: You're like all the rest. Congratulations. You failed all expectations.

(EDDIE suddenly lurches out of the room and staggers offstage USL. DRAKE comes onstage at the same point and stops abruptly to stare at the fleeing EDDIE.)

L.C. (*to himself*): He's so damned mean because he can't write anymore. This place didn't crap him out. He hasn't written 1000 good words in ten years. He could edit for a while. Proved that with his Paris memoirs. Now he can't even edit. So he's a sonuvabitch with handles. (*picks up phone and dials eight numbers*) Maggie Jones, please. Thank you. By God. Maggie was right. (*picks up book*) Pops wouldn't reread shit like this for all the gold in Switzerland. (*throws book down*) Maggie? Come on over. Pops just changed my mind again.

(DRAKE walks into his office as L.C. writes again in his notebook. L.C. scowls and pockets the notebook)

DRAKE: Mr. Rankin. (*gawks at closed drapes*) What was that all about?

L.C.: Mankin. (*waits, sees blank look and shrugs*) Pops thinks the parking lot is full of J. Edgars.

DRAKE: What?

L.C.: FBI agents.

DRAKE: He was teasing. (*opening the drapes*) Just a joke.

L.C.: No.

DRAKE: Have you changed your mind about the release?

63

L.C.: It would be handing him a gun.

DRAKE: The doctor he shoots skeet with says he is quite comfortable with guns. His father taught him to shoot a rifle when he was just two and a half. At four Edward Hathaway could handle a pistol.

L.C.: His father killed himself with a pistol!

DRAKE: I knew that.

L.C.: Did you know Maggie found him loading a gun just before he went into the hospital at Sun Valley?

DRAKE: He told me. He was cleaning the gun. Everyone over-reacted. Everyone was running as a crazy, he said.

L.C.: Did you read the suicide note?

DRAKE: I found that note ambiguous. It showed magnanimous concern for his wife.

L.C.: Did you know just before they flew him here he locked everybody out of the house and tried to load that same gun again?

DRAKE: He said he wanted to make sure it was not loaded.

L.C.: Did you know he tried to jump out of the plane they chartered?

DRAKE: It was a scuffle. He wasn't trying to jump. He is a proud man and he was being strong-armed.

L.C.: When they landed in Casper, he tried to run into the propeller.

DRAKE: He was disoriented. I concede he's only two-thirds well. But that's enough - IF he's surrounded by sympathetic friends.

L.C.: Did you know he tried to jump out of the plane a second time?

DRAKE: The truth is, Mr. Rankin, you weren't there to witness any of those alleged incidents. You speak as if you were. But you were not. Neither was Mrs. Hathaway.

L.C.: There were witnesses.

DRAKE: Well-meaning men out of their depth. Well-meaning men who panicked a man trying to cope with minor obsessions.

(MAGGIE trudges onstage USL, stops beyond French doors and straightens herself.)

L.C.: You better rip up those release papers, doctor. I may not have a medical degree but I do have substantial resources. I can reach a very large audience.

DRAKE: Are you threatening me?

L.C.: I promise I will have the entire incident printed. Start to finish. Front page. How much of your future are you willing to risk to see if Pops is well enough to leave?

(MAGGIE inhales and walks into the office.)

DRAKE: Mrs. Hathaway!

L.C.: Maggie. Sit down.

MAGGIE: I hope you have good news for me.

L.C.: Doctor? Do we?

DRAKE (*sighs*): Who is going to tell him?

L.C.: He won't listen to me or Maggie. We are part of the plot against him. You'll have to do our bidding.

MAGGIE: That's true.

DRAKE: He's strong willed.

L.C.: A couple of pills and he won't want to go anywhere.

MAGGIE: It makes me sick to think about tricking him like that but it's better than the other.

DRAKE: I don't like this. (*picks up phone*) I just don't.

L.C.: But you're handling the negotiations whether you like it or not. And you better handle them until he's well.

DRAKE (*dials four numbers*): Nurse? No, not yet! Listen. Give Edward Jones more pheno. I know it's a lot of trouble. Well, put it in his pudding again or something else he likes but do it!

MAGGIE: Thank God.

DRAKE: You can thank me. Nobody else is going to.

(L.C. stands as if an enormous weight is off him. MAGGIE embraces him.)

MAGGIE: L.C., thank you.

L.C.: Doctor, I expect to hear about a new series of ECTs.

DRAKE: I have a lunch engagement. (*looks at his watch*) Yes. It is almost twelve. Mr. Hathaway isn't leaving, so there's no big rush, is there? I'll talk to him after lunch.

(DRAKE walks out with the enthusiasm of a man on his way to face a firing squad. GRACE comes onstage USL and she and DRAKE huddle outside the French doors.)

MAGGIE: You will stay a few more days, won't you?

L.C.: The doctor understands supply and demand now.

MAGGIE: But shouldn't you wait a while?

(DRAKE trudges offstage USL. GRACE smiles maliciously and then exits USL.)

L.C.: There is not going to be a problem. The doctor understands this business now.

MAGGIE: I'm afraid. Eddie is so persuasive.

L.C.: My plane leaves at three-thirty. I've got to go to the hotel and pack my bags. Come on, Maggie. Have some lunch with me first. You're worrying over nothing. Not only is Pops staying but he's going to get the additional shock treatments you wanted and plenty of medication.

MAGGIE (*embraces L.C. again*): Thank God.

End of Act Two

ACT THREE

Eddie's room. Stage left is oblique wall with large French doors USL. The doors are open but partially blocked by the kind of baggage cart with a bar for hanging clothes. Nothing hangs on the bar. Near the wall DSR the desk is bare. The wheelchair is parked, facing into the corner USR, without the stuffed owl. The scraps of paper and photographs on the US wall are now mounded in one of two suitcases lying open on the hospital bed. Now uncovered on US wall is a picture of blue-eyed Jesus with blonde highlights in beard and shoulder-length hair. In front of closed drapes is the tray table on rollers. Both doors on the wall SR are open. The mass of toilet paper is on the floor in the closet DSR. Hangers on the bar in the closet are bare. EDDIE stands, peeking out the drapes.

EDDIE: Thicker than blue flies on the sphincter of a dead elephant. Goddamn it. Can't go. Can't stay. Finca gone. No boat in summer. Stretch gone. Goddamned few friends left now. Goddamn it! They are the lucky ones! Worst death for anyone is to lose the center of his being - the thing he really is. Can't write anymore. Too many ghosts too. I'm dead-house. Could solve everything with that heavy! Never liked that trigger. What the hell was big-bore bastard called? How could I forget a goddamned obscenity like that?

(EDDIE jumps back from the window.)

Five oh five Gibbs! Now why do I keep thinking of that
cannon? I'm not running as a cheerful. Black ass got that
Gibbs aiming at me off and on ever since lunch. (*looks
at wristwatch*) Two hours.

> (EDDIE walks to the bed and hunches over an open
> suitcase.)

By Christ, they cleaned me out fast. (*walks to closet and
picks up the mass of toilet paper*) Second part of three-
part story big enough to knock off Tolstoy and the
wrong person could send it to shit farm. (*walks back to
bed and tenderly arranges the paper in his suitcase*) Got
every thing but underwear which Grace knows I don't
own one pair of and other things which were cleaned out
fast.

GRACE (*enters USL and walks in*): Aren't you handy?
What do you think you are doing?

EDDIE: Where is my belt?

GRACE: Why are you packing those bags?

EDDIE: I'm clearing out. I'd rather drink monkey vomit
than die in this joint.

GRACE: Did you eat your lunch?

EDDIE: Sure. And I'm also missing...

GRACE: You don't act like you ate your lunch. Anyway,
Mr. Jones, you're not kissing off this place. Not yet.

EDDIE: Cows don't vote. Medico gave me true gen yesterday. Said release papers ready today. What did I say was missing?

GRACE (*viciously*): Well, you didn't hear the doctor right. You better just hump your behind down in your chair and relax, old man.

EDDIE: Papers not signed?

GRACE: You are not leaving for a while.

EDDIE: No problem. I waited for simba half a goddamned day with a tse-tse fly masticating my right testicle...

GRACE: You won't be leaving today!

EDDIE: And tomorrow and tomorrow and all tomorrows won't ever be today. (*sits on bed, very dejected*) By Christ, I'm stuck in this joint. (*holds out arm*) How about reading vessels?

GRACE: Can't you see I don't have the proper equipment?

(GRACE putters around and EDDIE rises and stands rigid, eyes blank, lost in thought. Suddenly he ducks as if someone threw a punch at his head.)

EDDIE: Goddamn it. Maybe just cornered. (*chops short left hook*)

GRACE: You relax. You've stroked your share. Now it's time to just relax. It's kind of like retiring.

EDDIE: Filthiest goddamned word in the language.

71

GRACE: I can't believe you ate your lunch. Did you eat your tapioca? Did Bertha give you those pills this morning?

EDDIE: Because genitals intact? Matter of fact, she didn't. Rarely does.

GRACE: I thought so! Will you tell Doctor Drake that?

EDDIE: After I tell you what I'm going to do about you.

GRACE: If that's a threat, old man, I'll rub your life raw.

EDDIE: By Christ, some women are awful. (*peeks out the drapes*) Sick in the head too. But any woman - even hell of a wonderful woman - can turn mean on a man although of course it is the man's own actions that turn her mean. If he leaves the woman though he probably ought to shoot her...

GRACE (*alarmed*): Shoot who?

EDDIE: ...but he can't do that on account of the children (*GRACE relaxes, shakes her head in disgust*) and so there is no solution actually to anything except to get so nobody can hurt him and by the time he does that he's probably been dead for some time. I wonder if I put that in a book.

GRACE: You definitely need to stay here where somebody can keep a thumb on you.

EDDIE: I'm going to make you my new Margot.

GRACE (*walks into bathroom USR, yells*): What are you talking about?

EDDIE: Short story.

GRACE (*still yelling*): I don't understand one word of your dumb stories.

EDDIE: Left too much out. This time won't leave too much out. Even for you.

GRACE (*reappears with cup, pulls vial out of uniform pocket*): Take these pills.

EDDIE: I'd sooner kiss the lips off a hyena. Listen once.

GRACE: Then speak English. You drool all those little words and I still can't understand you.

EDDIE: If I stay in this joint I jam you into a story with the doc. How you two are lovers and how the doc had to take care of a special problem for you once.

GRACE: How did...Bertha!

EDDIE: Thank you for confirming it.

GRACE: And if you get to blow this place?

EDDIE: If I leave to go home I forget about you - which will be easy because no interest in large breasts since weaned.

GRACE: You aren't writing anyway.

73

EDDIE (*grabs toilet paper*): Look at this!

> (GRACE sets cup and vial on the tray table and examines the paper like a scroll.)

Well?

GRACE (*drops the roll back in the suitcase*): None of this would have happened except for Bertha.

EDDIE: Padre told me too.

GRACE: No!

EDDIE: He's worried about you. You're not a hobby for him like I am. You're one of the flock.

GRACE: I never told you I was Catholic.

EDDIE: Who else would work at St. Martha's?

GRACE: So what if I am one? I heard you were too.

EDDIE: Not like you. You're special. For a priest.

GRACE: Because of the lie about my...my problem?

EDDIE: No, it's your calling. All priests are fascinated and helpless as moths before flame and worry and pray for what they imagine is their exact antithesis...a whore.

GRACE: Whore!

EDDIE: That's what I said.

GRACE: Well, this whore never wants to see your ugly red peeling face again.

EDDIE: Soon as I leave here I meet biggest whore of all.

GRACE: You sick old fool. Who would want to touch you?

EDDIE: I downsize those tumors and give you a brain to make you interesting to reader. Eight hundred words. Two days to set down in hot blood. A few more days to get the words right.

GRACE: Go to hell!

EDDIE: I can almost promise.

(PRIEST walks onstage USL, calmly watches GRACE run from the room. She stops, gives him a hateful look.)

GRACE (*as she exits USL*): You go to hell too!

(PRIEST enters the room.)

EDDIE: Just the Padre I have waited for.

PRIEST: What was all that...you're packing!

EDDIE: I'll be clear of this joint not long after the meridian.

PRIEST: That can't be. Not with your...your tendencies. I don't know what to do. I shouldn't tell anyone. But I should tell the doctor. But I really shouldn't tell anyone. But I have to tell...about your tendencies.

75

EDDIE: I liked it better when you were running as a silent. You won't tell any doctor.

PRIEST: But I must.

EDDIE: Like you must see little boys?

PRIEST: What!

EDDIE: I've seen a million corruptions like you hanging around bullfighters.

PRIEST: A million what?

EDDIE: Undeclared fairies.

PRIEST: Eddie! I'm not that way. I love men but not that way. I love...

EDDIE: I've seen a million. I hit a couple. They scream like girls.

PRIEST: But I'm not that way.

EDDIE: You wonder every day if you are that way. You fear you are because you never liked women. You fear people saying you are too. But I won't talk. And you won't be talking to any shock doctor about Edward Hathaway, who took you into the center of his being.

PRIEST: But I know why you want out.

EDDIE (*smiles and speaks in a prissy voice*): You needn't be superior.

PRIEST: That sounds....oh, no. Not that story!

EDDIE (*still prissy*): Go on and get on with whatever you were doing. Leave the door open when you go out.

PRIEST: That story!

EDDIE (*normal voice*): Bet you read it a thousand times. Bet you tremble under the covers at night thinking about it.

PRIEST: Only because I sorrow for lost souls...

(BERTHA storms onstage USL.)

EDDIE (*puttering with his suitcase*): Padre, you are slowing me down.

(BERTHA rushes into the room.)

I'm going to clear out of here fast.

BERTHA: Father!

EDDIE: If you stay, Padre, I will tell Bertha about bullfighters and the men who clap the loudest.

PRIEST: I'll pray for you. You can't stop me from doing that.

EDDIE: Goodbye, Padre. (*watches him leave, then puts his hands on his hips to face BERTHA, who has her hands on her hips too*) Four to one he wouldn't do it but I couldn't take the chance. (*sits on bed and pulls back sleeve*) Let's check the plumbing.

(PRIEST waits outside the French doors, very shaken. He is clearly trying to decide what to do.)

BERTHA: I aint checking nothing. I heard you thought you was leaving. I thought we was friends.

EDDIE: I did too until I started looking for my belt.

BERTHA: Did you tell Grace I wasn't feeding you your pills?

EDDIE: I meant you weren't shoving them down my throat with size twelve boots. Did she misinterpret?

BERTHA: She was way too mad for just some pill ducking. Did you say something about her special problem?

EDDIE: Never specified problem. Never said you said anything. Never used your hallowed name. (*crosses himself*) By all that's holy.

(PRIEST shakes his head, trudges offstage USL.)

BERTHA: You're lying. She definitely thinks I fed it to you.

EDDIE: A good writer has to lie. She acts awful though, doesn't she?

BERTHA: I sure didn't expect garbage like this from you.

EDDIE: Nor did I expect you to lift my belt.

BERTHA: What belt?

EDDIE (*jumps up from the bed*): Wasn't ten bucks enough
for the goddamned pencils and microscopic knife?

BERTHA: I never kept one crumb. I even spent some of
my own money...

EDDIE: How much dough did you get for the belt?

BERTHA: What belt?

EDDIE: My Gott Mit Uns belt.

BERTHA: I never heard of no belt like that.

EDDIE: Took it off a dead Kraut. God sure was with him,
wasn't he?

BERTHA: Mr. Jones, I think you should sit down again.

EDDIE: Let's get a reading. Goddamn belt was priceless.
What did you get? Five bucks? Now I remember! My
goddamned lucky chestnut. It's missing too, Bertha. I'm
going to have to report you.

BERTHA: Maybe you should go back to Idaho.

EDDIE: Now you're cutting through the bullshit.

(DRAKE comes onstage USL, with GRACE in
anguish at his elbow. She whispers in his ear.)

The sweet clean pull of a spring field. (*laughs*) Sweet
clean pull...

BERTHA: I don't know what slop you're trying to get me to swallow but I feel in my gut you're going to do something bad and as much as I can't stomach Drake I got to tell...

> (DRAKE pulls away from GRACE and storms into the room. GRACE smiles bitterly and watches.)

DRAKE: You won't tell anybody anything, nurse. See me in my office at four o'clock.

BERTHA: I just wanted to tell you...

> (Very pleased, GRACE exits USL.)

DRAKE: Nurse!

EDDIE: Best depart, Bertha.

> (BERTHA looks exasperated as she struggles to find the right words. She can't - and she trudges from the room to exit USL.)

DRAKE: Mr. Hathaway, you've been busy.

EDDIE: Good story not to deny.

DRAKE: Don't tell me you even crossed swords with Bertha?

EDDIE: She unbelted me, so I belted her. She even took my lucky...(*suddenly gropes in pants pocket*) No. Nut still there!

DRAKE: Even Father asked me to see you.

EDDIE: That seems to please you.

DRAKE: I was concerned about you and the priest. But obviously you just like to needle him. That's a good sign.

EDDIE: Because he's God-happy?

DRAKE: If you're packing to leave, Mr. Hathaway, I'm afraid you're premature.

EDDIE: I'm not clearing out of this joint?

DRAKE: I don't feel like we're quite ready yet.

EDDIE: Did nurse Grace tell you I am writing again?

DRAKE: I knew you were writing.

EDDIE: Did you?

DRAKE (*pulls some of the roll of paper from suitcase*): I didn't need to see this. I saw the shavings in your wastebasket. It was my goal to get you writing again.

EDDIE: Even if I write how doctor implants self in nurse. Short unhappy life of Grace's baby Drake.

DRAKE: You don't think much of me, do you?

EDDIE: The true gen on you is you have as much knowledge of the world as your miniature medico now supporting blades of grass in some lawn near here.

DRAKE: You can't goad me into doing the wrong thing.

EDDIE: Poise under pressure?

DRAKE: I'm certain now you need to stay here for more treatment.

EDDIE: I hope you haven't torn up the papers.

DRAKE: What papers?

EDDIE: For my release.

DRAKE (*feels his inside coat pocket*): The papers were never prepared.

EDDIE: I see.

DRAKE: I think you will stay a while longer, Mr. Hathaway. I have a lot to discuss with you.

EDDIE: Yes. We have a lot in common.

DRAKE: You think I've read none of your books?

EDDIE: You seem none the wiser.

DRAKE: Our nichts which art in nichts, nichts by thy name. Thy kingdom nichts. Thy will be nichts in nichts, as it is in nichts. Give us this nichts our daily nichts. And nichts us our nichts, as we nichts our nichts. And nichts us not into nichts, but deliver us from nichts...

EDDIE: And what does a psy-quackerist make of that?

DRAKE: There is no God. Nichts. Nothing. Naturally.

EDDIE: So I am now the patron of atheists?

DRAKE: In the Lord I put my trust; but not for long...

EDDIE (*to himself*): That was for a hypocrite.

DRAKE: It has your name on it.

EDDIE: Could the parodist of the eleventh Psalm run as anything but an atheist?

DRAKE: No. Naturally.

EDDIE: Let me see if I can remember all of this...
  Why art thou silent and invisible
  Father of jealousy?
  Why dost thou hide thyself in clouds
  From every searching eye?
  Why darkness and obscurity
  In all thy words and laws
  That none dare eat the fruit but from
  The wily serpent's jaws?

DRAKE: Beautiful.

EDDIE: Written by one of the greatest metaphysicists of all time.

DRAKE: Who wrote it?

EDDIE: Somebody to Nobodaddy.

DRAKE: Who?

EDDIE: Listen to this. Let me see if I can remember it...
  The vision of Christ that thou dost see
  is my vision's greatest enemy.
  Thine has a great hooknose like thine.
  Mine has a snub nose like to mine. (*salutes picture*)
  Thine is a friend to all mankind.
  Mine speaks in parables to the blind.

DRAKE: Beautiful. Who wrote it?

EDDIE: I suspect he was Manichean.

DRAKE: I'll remember that one. We're going to have some
  wonderful discussions, Mr. Hathaway.

EDDIE: Shall await your repartees with held breath - by
  sunlit mountain mailbox.

DRAKE: It is in losing that we become Christian...

EDDIE (*sighs and holds up his hand*): Don't tell me. That
  also has my name on it.

DRAKE: Christ wanted to cut and run on the cross...

EDDIE: That also has my name on it. (*sits on bed, very
  dejected*) I never knew how stupid a complete
  chickenshit might read my stuff.

DRAKE: The rest of the bunch cut and run...

EDDIE (*perks up*): Now we get to the central part of your
  being!

DRAKE: My being?

EDDIE: You run as a coward.

DRAKE: I'm no coward.

EDDIE: Where were you in second world war?

DRAKE: Medical school. I had every intention of going in.

EDDIE: But didn't.

DRAKE: They stopped the war without me.

EDDIE: How about Korea?

DRAKE: My occupation at home is critical for national defense.

EDDIE: Bet you got called up. Bet you took own prescription with eight cups of joe to jack blood pressure up to one ninety over one twenty. So far I've got you running as a murderer and a blasphemer and a coward!

DRAKE: Settle down, Mr. Hathaway. You can't goad me.

EDDIE: I've impaled and scalded with ink the very gods. Ford Madox Ford, Sinclair Lewis, Gertrude Stein, Max Eastman, Dorothy Parker, Harold Loeb, Archibald MacLeish, John dos Passos, James Joyce, Scott Fitzgerald, Faulkner and the list goes on and the stain is as permanent as the sun. If I ink you or get you into ink through an unwitting third party it will stick. If you really irritate me I will immortalize the diminutive size of your prick. I think I used that in a book once.

DRAKE: You're bluffing.

EDDIE: Don't worry. No one cares about your irrelevant prick. What else? Theft maybe? Incest?

DRAKE: You're grasping.

EDDIE: I want to get the true gen on this before I start writing.

DRAKE: Are you threatening me about writing?

EDDIE: Thought I could get you in eight hundred but see you might go eleven hundred. You took seven capital sins and ran up a record for mortal sins. Maybe invented one or two new ones.

DRAKE (*finally explodes, grabs the roll of paper and reads*): Think about God being, he thought. Think about Christ being. Think about Christ on the cross. Think about God on the cross. Think about Christ in the tomb. Think about God in the tomb. Think about God okay tonight. Think about God everywhere, all night. Think about God tomorrow. Think about Christ. God bless it, think about God...(*starts clawing and unrolling more paper*)

EDDIE: Never read my own stuff aloud. Did that once. Trusting and stupid as a bird dog. About as low as a writer can get and goddamned dangerous too.

DRAKE (*still reading*): Whether in the body, he thought, I can not tell. Think about it, he thought. Think about God knowing, he thought. Think about Christ knowing.

Think about whether was still in body or not, he thought. Think about God knowing. Think about coming back. Think about God knowing whether he came back. Think about back in body okay. Think about God and unspeakable words. Think about God all night...(*stops again and claws at the paper to unroll more*)

EDDIE: Never made third heaven. Goddamn close though. I came right out of my body, like a silk handkerchief pulled out of a pocket by one corner. Flew all around and then came back and went in again and wasn't dead any more.

DRAKE (*still reading*): They think they are masters of the word? Think about it, he thought. I think I am more than they are. More words, more wars, more wounds, often near death. Five times took head wounds because of Krauts, three times machine-gunned, once mortared, two times jeep wrecked, spent a day and a night with ruptured kidneys; often on road, danger from rivers, danger from collaborators, danger from my own people, danger from foreigners, danger in the city, danger in the wilds, danger at sea, danger among crooks; with toil and hardship, often sleepless, in hunger and thirst, often famished, cold and naked. Aside from externals was day-by-day pressure...

EDDIE: Goddamn bad some times.

DRAKE: Mr. Hathaway, this is just toilet paper.

EDDIE: Had to make do.

DRAKE: My specific point is it's still nothing but toilet paper.

EDDIE: Can get eleven hundred words. Might take me six months but can get it.

DRAKE: Think you have six months?

EDDIE: One sentence a day. Short and true. Can do. Even in this joint. Can smuggle it outside this joint too. You try to stop me. I can get it outside. I can get anything published. I could get my goddamned pulse published.

DRAKE: You will stay. You can bully the nurses. Maybe you can get a couple of them dismissed but...

EDDIE: Drake. Can't use Drake. How about Pilate? P-I-L-A-T-E? Too direct. Maybe Helms. Get it? Helmsman. Pilot, P-I-L-O-T? Homophone is P-I-L-A-T-E. By Christ, I didn't say it would be easy.

DRAKE (*pulls the papers out of his inside pocket*): You knew I had these.

EDDIE: I'll take those, thank you.

DRAKE: You can't bully me. I'm going to tear them up.

EDDIE: Grace. Can't use Grace. Need name of nurse cum whore. Can't use Catherine. Gives dignity to nurse with none. I know. Herodias, Herod's whore. Rodias. Rhoda. No.

DRAKE: You can use Grace a thousand times for all I care. I'm going to tear the papers up.

EDDIE: More whores in Old Testament. Rahab. Tough name to work with. But make do. What is your mother's name?

DRAKE: My mother? Now listen...

EDDIE: Need name.

DRAKE: You can flat go to hell!

EDDIE: Can find out name. Easy. One buck plus one lie equals Doc Drake birth certificate.

DRAKE: This is not funny.

EDDIE: If you read me you know I am not funny, doc. You will wake up to noise in middle of every night. But picking and scraping and hammering and shoveling night after night after night that chills your blood is not Roman legions in siege. No. It's old Edward Hathaway jamming dirt on Portable Corona Number Three into story of third-rate babykilling psy-quackerist.

DRAKE: You would never do it.

EDDIE: You're running a very big gamble. Money machine of young shock doctor on the line to detain old wreck of a writer.

DRAKE: I said you couldn't goad me.

EDDIE: Will go one light year beyond goading. Maybe go to one lifetime of ridicule.

DRAKE: I still won't do it.

EDDIE: Eleven hundred true words has Shock Doctor Helms who yellowed out of the war impregnating Nurse Rachel Habb and doc wrestles with conscience based on Burma Shave signs and repeated incest with yet to be named mother which caused him to run when kid brother was drowning in pond which he relives as he watches bleeding fetus extracted from Rachel swirl down vortex of toilet.

DRAKE (*sick*): It's all a lie based on a malicious rumor. God.

> (MAGGIE and L.C. hurry onstage USL, obviously frantic.)

EDDIE: Too cowardly to invoke him. You forfeited your rights anyway. Surrender papers on bed!

> (MAGGIE and L.C. burst into the room as DRAKE places the papers on the bed.)

L.C. (*picks up papers*): What is going on here? (*to DRAKE*) You reneged!

DRAKE (*ignores L.C.*): I didn't send for you, Mrs. Hathaway. But it's a good thing you came anyway.

MAGGIE: We heard we might be needed.

EDDIE: Thought I knocked out all bridges. One bridge still intact.

MAGGIE: Doctor, just what is happening here?

DRAKE: I've had a long talk with Mr. Hathaway.

EDDIE: We understand each other. (*snatches papers from L.C.*) Like old comedy team of Helms and Habb.

MAGGIE: Eddie, are you packing to leave?

EDDIE: Affirmed.

MAGGIE: Eddie, lamb, you can't leave.

L.C.: God no. Doctor, I thought everything was square with you.

DRAKE: Mr. Hathaway is writing again.

EDDIE: Eleven hundred on a good day.

MAGGIE: What is all that toilet tissue?

L.C.: My God. It is covered with writing.

DRAKE: I said he is writing again.

EDDIE: I'm pretty beat up but I can still write.

MAGGIE: Stay here then and write, lamb.

L.C.: Nobody to mess with the firm here, Pops. We'll get you reams of good typing paper.

EDDIE: Medicos are cramping me.

MAGGIE: Eddie, stay.

L.C.: God yes.

EDDIE: Can't write when nurse shoving bed pan under ass. (*stuffs paper back in bag and closes bag*) Leaving here is about like getting bounced from a leper colony.

MAGGIE: You can't do this. Somebody do something!

L.C.: We're just in the home stretch is all. We'll see a judge.

DRAKE: I've done all I can for him now.

EDDIE (*walking to the window*): Got a lot to do. Going to be busier than a one-armed South Korean.

MAGGIE: Somebody do something!

EDDIE (*peeking through drapes*): By Christ! Coast clear!

> (EDDIE grabs bag with toilet paper and rushes to French doors, but abruptly stops. Gropes in pants pocket and pulls out chestnut.)

> Double dicho, L.C. Writer can never be destroyed but writer's work can be destroyed.

> (EDDIE slaps chestnut into L.C.'s hand and never looks back as he exits USL.)

MAGGIE: What are we going to do?

DRAKE: I'm sorry. Legally...

MAGGIE: He has no money!

L.C.: Edward Hathaway needs no money. He is money.

DRAKE: Legally, I just couldn't detain him.

MAGGIE: We've got to do something!

L.C.: Writer's work can never be destroyed but...(*suddenly opens hand to look at the chestnut and yells*) writer can be!

MAGGIE: What's that?

L.C.: His double dicho. Let's go.

(L.C. rushes from the room and quickly exits USL.)

MAGGIE: What about his medication?

DRAKE (*sees vial and walks to tray table*): This is enough for a while. One every six hours. I'll call your druggist in Idaho to make sure you have more. (*hands her the vial*) Liquid and tablets.

MAGGIE: But what if he won't take it?

DRAKE: He has to eat.

MAGGIE (*almost frantic*): Wait! What did that priest say about his medication? Something all twisted. Black is white and white is black.

DRAKE: I don't remember.

>   (MAGGIE lingers a moment, agitated and confused,
>   then suddenly bolts out the doors and exits USL.)

There was nothing I could do. Legally. (*suddenly smiles*)
Goodbye forever, Mr. Hathaway.

End of Play

www.ingramcontent.com/pod-product-compliance
Lightning Source LLC
Chambersburg PA
CBHW070510130626
46555CB00003B/1232